HARRY
and the
Lady Next Door

HARRY

by Gene Zion

Pictures by
Margaret Bloy Graham

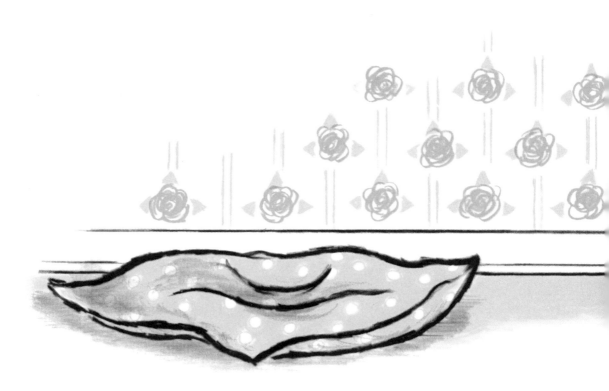

An I Can Read
Picture Book™

and the Lady Next Door

BARNES & NOBLE

NEW YORK

Barnes & Noble Publishing, Inc.
122 Fifth Avenue
New York, NY 10011

ISBN 0-7607-6504-9
Manufactured in China
08 09 MCH 10 9 8 7 6 5

CONTENTS

THE PARTY

Harry was a white dog with black spots.

He loved all his neighbors, all except one.

He did not love the lady next door.

The lady next door sang. She sang high and loud.

When she sang, Harry's ears hurt.

She sang higher than the peanut whistle. When she sang,

the peanut man put his hands over his ears.

She sang louder than the siren on the fire engine.

When she sang, the firemen put their hands

over their ears.

She sang higher and louder than the cats sang.

When she sang, the cats ran away.

Harry tried everything to make her stop. He howled
under her window. His friends howled too.
But it did not do any good. The lady next door
went on singing. She sang higher and louder than ever.

One day Harry's family gave a party. They invited

the lady next door. She came with her music.

When she started to sing, Harry almost bit

her leg. But he bit the leg of the piano instead.

The family sent Harry out of the room. "You are

a bad dog," they said. Harry just wagged his tail.

As he walked to the door some people said,

"Poor Harry." But others whispered,

"The lucky dog!"

When Harry pushed the door open the wind blew in.

It blew the pages of music off the piano.

They blew all around the room.

Everyone tried to catch the music but no one could.

The pages blew out the door and into the garden.

They blew over the fence and up into the trees.

Harry caught some of the pages but he did not

bring them back. He ran away with them.

HARRY'S FIRST TRY

He ran until he came to a quiet spot. He dropped

the music and lay down. Soon he fell asleep.

In a little while something woke Harry up.

All around him were cows mooing. They mooed

very low notes. Harry listened.

He thought the cows made beautiful music.

He had never heard anything so soft and low.

He wished the lady next door would sing like the cows.

Suddenly Harry had an idea.

He rounded up all the cows. He barked at their heels.

Down the road they went. Harry barked and the cows mooed.

They ran on and on. They ran down the main street of town.

They passed the school, the library and the fire house.

When they came to Harry's house the lady was still singing.

Harry ran ahead and stopped the cows. They went on mooing.

They mooed and mooed and mooed.

They all mooed soft and low. The cows mooed for a long time but it did not do any good. The lady next door went on singing. She sang higher and louder than ever.

Harry's family called the man who owned the cows.

He came and took them home.

That night Harry slept in the dog house.

HARRY'S SECOND TRY

The next day the lady next door sang some more.

Harry's ears hurt more than ever. He went for a walk.

After he had walked for a long time

he heard a wonderful sound.

"Oompah! Oompah! Oompah! Oompah!"

It was low and lovely.

Then Harry saw what it was. It was the big horn
in the Firemen's Band. The big horn was even softer
and lower than cows mooing. Harry walked along listening.

He wished the lady next door would sing like the big horn.

Then he saw the leader of the band. The leader threw his stick

into the air. Harry watched. Suddenly he had an idea.

The next time the stick went into the air Harry caught it.

Harry ran in front of the band. The leader ran after Harry—

and the band ran after the leader.

Soon the leader was all out of breath. He stopped running.

But the band ran after Harry. The men played as they ran.

Harry led them all down the main street of town.

They passed the school, the library and the fire house.

Harry stopped the band in front of the lady's house.

She was still singing. The big horn player played

even softer and lower than before.

He blew and blew and blew right under her window.

But it did not do any good. The lady next door

went on singing. She sang higher and louder than ever.

When the leader got there he had Harry's family with him.

Harry gave the stick back.

That night he slept in the dog house again.

THE CONTEST

A few nights after that, the family took Harry to the park.

They were going to hear the Firemen's Band.

The family knew that Harry liked the big horn.

They got to the park and sat down. A light shone

on the stage. The people were quiet. They waited

for the music to begin. Harry closed his eyes and listened.

He waited for the big horn.

He waited for the soft, low notes.

But the low notes never came. Instead, a man came out. "Good evening, friends," he said. "The band will not play tonight. The big horn player is all out of breath. Instead we shall have a singing contest. And here are the ladies who will sing."

Everyone clapped when the ladies came out. On the end
of the line was the lady next door. Harry took one
look and ran off.

He was almost out of the park when he heard something.

"Blurp Blurp."

"Blurp Blurp."

It was low and beautiful.

Harry stopped and listened. It was even softer

and lower than the cows and the big horn.

He wished the lady next door would sing like this.

Then he saw where the sound came from. It came from

inside a watering can. Suddenly Harry had an idea.

He took the handle of the can in his mouth.

Then he ran with it.

When he got back to the bandstand,

he walked quietly up the stairs.

The lady next door was singing.

Harry put the watering can on the floor behind her.

Soon the lady sang a *very* high note. Then something

happened. Two frogs jumped out of the can. One jumped

on the lady's head. The other jumped on her shoulder.

The other ladies in the contest shrieked and ran

from the stage. But the lady next door went on singing.

She sang higher and louder than ever.

When she finished her song everyone shouted, "Hooray!"

The judges whispered together. Then one of them spoke.

"Ladies and gentlemen," he said. "The other ladies

in the contest have all gone home. So the lady next door

wins the singing contest! She is a *brave* lady.

She wins First Prize. It means she can study music

in a far-off country for a long time!"

Everyone clapped and clapped. Harry barked and barked.

He was the happiest of all.

In the middle of all the fuss the frogs hopped home.

Soon the time came for the lady next door to go away.

Harry went to the ship with the family to see her off.

"Good-bye! Good-bye!" everyone shouted. Harry wagged his tail.

The lady next door started to sing

a good-bye song. But no one ever heard her.

Just as she sang the first note

the ship blew its foghorn.

It was a deep, low, wonderful sound. As the ship moved away from the dock, other boats blew their foghorns too. Harry thought it was the most beautiful good-bye song he had ever heard.

THE END